CHAPTER ONE

HALLIE

"Way too sexy for this office."

"For our own good." That came from the captain, I thought. Hux, maybe?

"Shouldn't be allowed." One of the plebs. Drayson. Grayson? Someone new to the team, mouthing off.

"Fuckkkkk..."

The communal groan went up as my office manager bent over at the water cooler, presenting her peach-shaped, and completely office inappropriate mini skirt clad behind to the ogling masses that made up the main cohort of the Jericho Chimeras Ice Hockey pro team.

The WAGS congregated about someone's underutilized desk in the main front office of the home team building—no, not for *that* purpose—situated in the corner giggled. They usually did over any random muscled member of the team no matter who they were attached to at the time. Someone, I didn't lift my head from the tower of marketing proofs scattered across my desk, you know, *work,* to check on who, broke off from the group and clicked their patent heels over the tiled flooring and sauntered across to the cooler. Then the heel did a little double tap and I sighed.

Janelle. It had to be. The office manager had always wanted to be on team WAG. She'd dropped a lot of weight recently and she'd been flirting up a storm with the team captain at every opportunity, too. Even I couldn't ignore that.

Right on cue the captain's deep voice filled the office alongside Janelle's giggle.

It looked like the chattering, sashaying WAGS ranks were about to swell with one more member.

Not that I'd ever want to be one, thank you very much.

My glasses slid down my nose a fraction as I studied the blurring words on the pages before me. I shuffled the papers and blinked rapidly, but the new view didn't change anything. I'd been staring at the

PUCK ME SIDEWAYS

A JERICHO CHIMERAS STALKER HOCKEY DARK
ROMANCE

JERICHO CHIMERAS

SOFIA AVES

First Edition

PAPERBACK ISBN 978-1-922448-99-6

EBOOK ISBN 978-1-923471-00-9

Working alongside the hottest hockey team is her dream-right up until the most droolworthy goalie on the ice does the one thing that ruins all her dreams. He notices her.

Hallie Newman has spent the last four months at the home of the Jericho Chimeras pretending not to exist. After all, the curvy marketing graduate knows exactly what it feels like to have her heart broken by a pro hockey player, and stomped all over by a puck bunny WAG wannabe.
But when she finds herself in Solace Hunter's sights he leaves her no room to escape—and he's been watching her for longer than anyone knows.

Because Hallie is his obsession. And just like his job as goalie for the Chimeras, Solace takes the protection of what he considers his seriously-and he's already claimed Hallie whether she knows it or not.

proofs for way too freaking long, and I needed a break. But getting up in front of the team was premeditated social, as well as personal suicide, and I liked my life.

Kind of. Mostly.

Liar, liar, marketing proofs on fire.

That was me. Hallie Newman, marketing pleb for the best ice hockey team in the south.

Only, it might have been a better idea fangirling from afar than actually working side by side with some of the team. Or all of them. Because so much of that glam-fangirl-glitter wore off so fast that I couldn't keep up four months into a job I loved or hated, depending on the minute. This was definitely a mood career.

"You know you're sexier than all of them put together."

I blinked at my papers and reshuffled them, trying to figure out where the voice came from. A shadow obscured my light—a really big freaking shadow. I stared right up into a pair of dark eyes the entire country knew belonged to Solace Hunter, the Chimera's defender. Goalie. Whatever.

Loyal to his team, unmoveable to a fault. And vicious to anyone who got on his other side.

Because I saw that when he belted the crap out

of a guy who decided to key his captain's car the first night I worked late and locked up, thinking I was still alone in the building.

Thank God he didn't see *me*, because who knows what he would have done to the witness when he dragged the guy's unconscious form to the back of his sports car, threw him in the trunk, and drove away.

I never mentioned the incident afterward. Some long dormant survival instinct kicked in. The next day the captain's car was fixed, and the guy's existence just never came up.

I managed to stay well away from Solace Hunter, Chimera defender after that...until right now. Coal dark eyes stared down at me, not a flicker of amusement or flirtation in sight.

Because Solace *didn't* flirt.

Like the rest of his actions, everything was done with a potent degree of determination. He was often the first Chimera in the gym working out in the mornings and the last to leave at night, checking the building when he thought no one remained.

I knew, because those quiet hours were when I got my best work done. When no one bothered me. The empty building left me quiet time to deal with the chatter my desk screamed at me that I couldn't deal with during the day in an overpopulated, over sensory office. Plus, knowing Solace was around offered a kind of safety.

I mean, who would screw with a guy like *that?*

No one. Certainly not this girl.

Lost in my head, I stared up at him and managed to swallow on a dry throat. "Huh?"

Cute, Hallie. Real smart, right there.

Solace smirked, though something impossibly dark flickered behind his eyes as he leaned in closer. "You really don't pay attention to the bull-shit out there, do you?" he murmured, sweeping a hand almost triple the size of mine out to encompass the rest of the room where I still refused to look.

I didn't want to see the faces that wouldn't look down at me, anyway. Or worse, gawk back at the shitshow that was about to go down.

Heat climbed my throat, heading for my cheeks. I didn't want to know where it originated, especially when this man had been the centre of too many late night fantasies that should never have been a part of my spank bank repertoire.

Because Solace Hunter was so far out of my league it wasn't funny. We shouldn't share the same building, let alone the same breathing space. My fingers shook the tiniest fraction as I pushed my glasses back up my nose where they drooped.

"I don't really fit in over there." I matched his soft tone, unwilling to bring more attention my way, and doubly unsure why I bothered to engage him.

This conversation wouldn't end well. For me, at least.

For Solace...I was just another girl he'd shrug off. He must have puck bunnies flying out every orifice on a daily basis. Those shoulders could lift a small planet, and he had abs to support everything above that, plus all the accompanying pucking bits...I should know. I got to stare at all the promo shots on a daily basis and make sure everyone's other bits—titles, names, and stats—were presented correctly.

If perving was a perk, I would rank out in the next employee satisfaction survey on that topic alone. Hell, I probably knew their numbers better than half the players did themselves.

"You're right." He didn't straighten, still invading my space and continued this Godforsaken conversation that headed exactly nowhere. "You don't fit in there."

"Exactly. So. Work." I let out a controlled breath and dropped my gaze back to my desk, shuffling my proofs—yet again—out of order to give myself something to do because what *did* a fangirl do when a hulking behemoth mountain of hockey sex god leaned over one's desk?

Answer: shuffle the proofs like a Vegas card counter, and pray for absolution.

"Like I said, you're sexier than all of them. Any one of them." He refused to budge.

I bit my lip, squeezing my eyes shut. "I know you get whoever you want, Solace. I know you have loads of time in the middle of the day between training sessions, and I *know* you work your ass off. Maybe you could, you know...let me do some of that last right now, too?" I bit back the *please* that teetered on the tip of my tongue, because begging with this man seemed wrong. Dangerous, even.

His breath huffed against the back of my neck when he laughed softly. "This is what makes you sexy, Hallie. Unlike them, you understand what a work ethic is. It's fucking beautiful." His fingers trailed lightly along my spine to my nape beneath my shoulder length dark hair and rested there, the touch hidden from sight to anyone else. *Intimate.* "Like you. This brain is the prettiest damn thing in here."

I swallowed hard and pushed my chair back, but his bulk blocked me in. "Let me up," I breathed, my heart hammering in my chest as the room shrank on me. "We— I'm just the marketing pleb. I can't do this. I'll lose my job."

"You can't be told you're beautiful?" He massaged my neck in gentle circles. The callouses and strength in his massive fingers belied by the sweetness of his touch.

My body ached for that touch. Craved it. I hadn't had contact with another person, anyone actually, apart from my cat, since—

Nope. Not going there.

"I have an aversion to puck bunnies." That's what fell out of my mouth as one of the WAGS headed in our direction. One without a flashy diamond ring on her finger, which, in my limited experience, was the most dangerous sort.

A black Chimera branded coffee mug stamped with her name that I forgot the moment I read it slammed down on my desk along with a few loose strands of bleached, split hair. "Coffee, honey. Black. Nothing in it. Just give me the dregs today. It's all in the effort of...you know." She shimmied at my desk while I tried not to look at her.

My chin dipped down in an effort to hide. My camouflage. It's how I'd survived in the months since I started. *Don't talk to anyone, don't make eye contact.*

Pretend you're not one of them. Because I wasn't. I made that mistake in my first week on the job, starting out friendly. Hell, did I get an education in all the things I was *not* in those first five working days that made me question my sanity, my entire career plan and my life choices. But I returned the following Monday with a new plan, and I'd stuck to it ever since.

Hence, my survival in my role as not-a-WAG and bottom-line marketing pleb. I sighed, pushed my proofs into an incomprehensible pile that would take half an hour after they all departed to sort back out, and grabbed the Chimeras mug presented to me.

"Sure, Cindy."

The WAG flared mid-shimmy. "My *name* is–"

"She doesn't care what your goddamn name is, Mindy," Solace snapped, corded arms straining beneath his shirt as he braced his fists knuckle first on my desk and towered over both of us.

Now that is a sexy sight.

I mentally added to my spank bank as Cindy-Mindy preened while I cowered. If I played dead, he'd forget I existed, right?

Nope. One inked hand returned to its place on the back of my neck. The fingers tightened when

Cindy-Mindy didn't move from her place before my desk. I stared at the mug, willing everyone to leave. Well, maybe not quite *everyone*. Tension emanated from the Chimera who held me pinned to my desk chair and drew me out of my camouflage-slump.

"Don't you dare get up," he growled at me darkly when I trembled like a freaking victim.

No sound came out of my mouth when it fell open, because what else could I be beneath hands that size?

He switched his attention forward, his tone hardening. "She's not your fucking doormat. Go back and play with things at your own level," he snapped at the WAG throwing her tits in his face.

I didn't think she was attached to him, but then I never paid attention to the revolving door of the Chimera WAG squad anyway.

"Okay," I breathed, unsure who I answered.

Cindy-Mindy huffed and flounced off, snatching her mug back from my fluttering hands. Her razored talons in the same lurid fuchsia—at least they aren't gold—that lit her name in neon on the mug grazed my fingers hard enough to draw twin lines of red along my fingers.

"Sit up," Solace ordered.

I squiggled about in my seat, craning back at an

uncomfortable angle to find his face. "You're ridiculously tall," I informed him.

The hard lines around his mouth eased a fraction. "And you're tiny."

I laughed at him, loud enough to turn heads, but then who hadn't just heard that little office level domestic? The rumor mill would be in full swing after that, anyway. I discarded my brand of camouflage and did something different for once.

Solace brought out a part of me I'd kept hidden, apparently. He made me feel...reckless.

"I'm so far from tiny it's not funny," I giggled, taking off my glasses to swipe at the tears gathering at the corners of my eyes, and gestured at my curved tummy. That one curved out, not in. No concave bits on this girl.

"Stop," he ordered again.

I froze and looked up at him curiously. "Do people always do what you say because you say it?" I asked politely.

His mouth twitched. "Yes. But not you, apparently." He caught my wrist and liberated my glasses, cleaning them absently on the hem of his numbered shirt. His eyes roamed over my face, then he placed them gently back on the bridge of my nose. Fingers traced my hair, flicking it out from behind my ear. He nodded decisively. "Nah. So much better on."

I wasn't sure if my stomach was in freefall, or if he just offered me a backhanded compliment. "Thanks?" I opted for a dry tone.

The small smile was back. He leaned in until his lips grazed my ear and my temperature spiked.

"Sexy as fuck, Hallie."

Then the Jericho Chimeras behemoth of a defender straightened, his face clean of emotion. Solace Hunter wandered away like nothing just happened between us at all.

CHAPTER TWO

SOLACE

The puck slid across the ice in front of Huxley Radfield like the damn thing was made of candy floss. I set myself to defend the signature slap shot he'd set up. Despite the action in front of me, my mind kept drifting to the pretty little dark haired temptation working in the main office who shouldn't be such a distraction. And yet, she was.

"Heads up, Hunter!" Coach yelled.

I heard him a fraction too late. The puck slammed past me into the net before I managed to raise my stick.

I swore liberally at myself while nodding to my captain. "Great set up, Hux. Saw it coming, but I know your style."

"Pity you didn't do anything about it." He removed his helmet, and frowned. "That obvious?"

"Yeah, but I've been playing side by side with you for three years, my man."

He nodded, his mouth set in a tight line. "If you see it, so will the opposition. Try to keep an eye on the puck and out of whatever pussy you were daydreaming about, alright?"

Ah, fuck.

I cast Hallie as far to the back of my mind as I could banish her for the moment, apologizing liberally to the girl I'd harbored a long running dark as fuck fantasy for, and promised myself I'd notch it up a level soon. Getting close to her earlier in the week brought out something in me I hadn't felt for a damn long time.

Maybe I'd come to the end of my long tease with myself. Maybe I'd broken my own rules by touching her.

Maybe I was full of shit.

"Bring your worst, Cap." I tightened my pads, nodding to Coach.

He watched me without smiling.

Damn. I had to prove my worth to both of them today. My little playtime would have to wait. I had a job to do first.

My muscles ached after the beating I gave myself on the ice, but Hux never got another goal past me for the rest of the session. I'd suitably redeemed myself in both his eyes and Coach's, though I hadn't yet forgiven myself for the slip. Now the rest of the team —and all but one person—had left for the night, I was free to let my mind run through all the things I wanted to do to the girl I'd banished from my mind earlier.

Hallie Newman had no idea the effect she had on the entire office. She was the sexiest thing I'd ever seen, and prettier after the sun set when everyone vacated the office for their pithy lives for the night.

That dark head of curls held not only my attention, but every eye in the team and over half the WAGS who usually paid less attention to others than anything else. Their pretence at vagueness was limited to the range of their significant other, and not an inch further—until it came to Hallie.

On a bet, it'd be because I'd taken an interest and shown her attention. I should have been more wary of the predators she went out of her way to protect herself against. The way she curled in on herself at her desk even when I was there, like she expected me to either ignore her or go along with the whole bullshit act, set something alight low in my gut.

Hell, I hadn't had the foresight to realize how bad the bullying got until I watched Mindy demean her in front of me, like she was the office joke.

Not on my fucking watch.

And I'd been watching little Miss Hallie since the day she arrived in the Chimera's office months ago. The marketing *pleb* in her words, who thought no one saw her. But I noted the hours she worked late, even if her boss never did.

What she didn't know was that I then waited for her to leave and shadowed her to the bus stop. Every single night. It became my new routine, instead of heading to the club with the rest of the team who typically got drunk off their asses and laid by whichever puck bunny was available if their chosen WAG wasn't in attendance. I hated that culture with a passion and refused to participate, preferring my own stalkerish tendencies for company.

Which made tonight exceptional as I decided to wait beside the front door after I locked up for the night until my pucking little prey decided to pack it in and emerge from the building. While she took her sweet time, working through whatever it was she needed the quiet hours for, I rested my head back against the wall beside the door and planned out my approach.

Well, hers, because I'd be the first thing she saw the moment she stepped out into the night. I didn't peg my little Hallie as a screamer, but I was ready for that too, prepared to wrap my hand around her mouth and pull her into my body until her chest stopped heaving, and the muffled sounds eased.

Just the thought of her struggle made me hard. I swallowed back the need to yank open the damn door, storm into the office and find out how well the two of us fit on her desk. No, waiting was sweeter. The tease left the sort of edge I craved, what I ached for. Getting off meant nothing without it.

Fast satisfaction and then...what? Nothing. No more than a drunk puck bunny in a back alley.

No, taking Hallie would be a slow process. Tease and back off. Tempt her and see how she reacted, all the while heightening both our arousal. I was far from immune to the way she responded to my touch at her desk a few days before. This morning's training session ended in a shit show where I couldn't focus on anything but her no matter how much I denied the vision of her.

I might have redeemed myself to Coach, but Shannon Incarsen owned my ass, the moment he and Hux turned their backs. Thankfully he was the only one who noticed my distraction for the rest of the training session.

I sank into my headspace for tonight as lights flicked off inside. Hell, I could almost scent her before she appeared, only a thin wall separating us, though she didn't know I waited on her yet. *Good.*

Her hand pressed to the glass door, pushing it open as I slipped my hands into my pockets, leaving my eyes half open, savoring the moment.

Cue scream in three, two, one...

"Jesus fucking *Christ–*" she muttered, slapping my chest with her habitual stack of manilla folders I swore she'd pulled straight out of the nineties. "The hell are you doing out here, stalking me?"

I snorted and stared down at her, leaving my eyes half lidded. "Exactly that, beautiful. Stalking you." I pulled one hand from my pocket and traced over her parted lips that looked too much like an invitation I wanted to take. I kept expecting some rebuke, but nothing came from her lips except a soft breath that brushed my fingertips. "You have a filthy mouth, you know that? I think I like it." My cock twitched as my chest ached. "Violent and sassy. Two of my favourite things."

She glared at me and pulled her head away,

retreating as she headed toward the bus stop and dismissed me. "Whatever. Go home, Solace. Are you drunk?"

I loped along beside her, keeping pace easily as her shorter legs took two steps to my one. "I don't drink. You know that."

A small noise I instantly loved escaped her. "Yes, I know that," she admitted in a voice that carried, even though I suspected she didn't intend that to happen. "What are you doing?" She stopped walking and turned to face me.

"Damn, girl. You've got some reflexes."

I pivoted just in time to prevent from over-shooting her position and grazed my palm over her elbow—not exposed, because hardly any of her could be seen. I always loved that about her. Unlike the regular WAG crew, Hallie kept herself covered up. It just made me want to peel those layers of clothing from her body to get to the soft, sumptuous curves underneath, and she had plenty of those.

Or maybe rip her layers right off.

Yeah, that'd be more fun. See if she made more of those little sounds.

"Stop chasing me." Exasperation creased her brow as she started walking again, a touch slower this time.

I knew she wasn't a fast walker, because I kept pace with her most nights. Just...not this close.

And being this close was a heady damn thing.

"I wanted to walk you to your bus." I shrugged like it was a normal thing. Not stalkerish at all.

Which, of course, it wasn't.

She rolled her eyes. "I knew you were there, Solace. When you walked behind me each night. Every night. You're not half as stealthy as you think."

I coughed into my fist. "Well, shit." I risked a look at her sideways. "You angry with me?"

Hallie let one shoulder rise and fall. "I mean, as long as you're not beating the crap out of me and loading me into the back of your trunk and towing me away, I guess it's kinda sweet. Like I felt safer knowing you were there."

That one earned her a choking sound like a dying fucking llama. I hadn't realized anyone saw me that night. Hell, she could have gotten herself hurt or worse if our vandal had a crew about and I hadn't been there to handle him.

"Jesus, girl. Beautiful, smart, and ballsy. Is there anything you can't do?" I stopped and gripped her upper arm, pulling her to face me sharply as I frowned. When she didn't struggle, I yanked her into my chest because I *needed* her to know I wasn't half as safe as she seemed to believe. "Actually, scratch that. Do you really think telling someone you saw them attack another man when you're alone at night with no one damn well around is smart? There's no one fucking well here, Hallie." I gestured to the sparsely lit area around us.

It was one of the reasons I spent the last months following her at night. One of. The rest weren't half as chivalrous.

She shrugged. *Shrugged.* "Probably not."

My grip tightened as I arched over her. "You should be screaming," I warned her softly.

Hallie stared up at me, her dusky pink lips parted the way they did at her desk. I wanted to bruise them with my mouth, push my tongue inside and find out how wet and hot she was.

Catalogue her taste.

"I didn't think you'd want someone noisy," she whispered.

My cock thickened painfully in my jeans. "So if I pushed you back against that building and found all those soft, sensitive spots on your body I've fucking dreamed about, what sort of noises would you make for me then, Hallie?" I growled, pulling her flush against my body so she could feel every tortured inch of my need.

Her breaths came fast and shallow, matching my own pants. Fuck, we were both halfway gone already. This was beyond dangerous, and not part of the plan at all.

"You've dreamed of me?" she whimpered, confusion twisting her plump lips.

Pressure built in my chest that matched the rumble of her bus rocketing along the street adjacent to us. I could put her in my car and take her home, but that would be a terrible fucking idea right now.

"Go, Hallie. Run," I murmured. "I'll wait, make sure you're safe."

She shook her head, blinking slowly at me as the world seemed to register back at her, and then her feet were moving as she flurried toward her bus, her hand raised as she called out. The vehicle slowed. She climbed on, her arms wrapped around herself and her collection of ever present folders she clutched like a shield that wouldn't protect her from me or anything else.

I watched her move halfway along the bus, staying exactly where I was, though she never looked back as she found a seat and sat with her back to me. I kept watching until I couldn't see her anymore, then pulled out my phone and used the number I stole from the office when she first arrived.

Solace: *Tell me when you get home or I'm coming to find you.*

I waited a solid minute for a reply and when there wasn't one, I sent the next message.

Solace: *I don't play games, Hallie. I need to know you get home safe.*

The next ten minutes were utter torture as I perched my ass on the hood of my car and waited, flipping my phone over in my hand. Finally, a message buzzed through. Certain she would tell me where to go, I found myself looking at a forlorn, gray cat adorned with wet whiskers.

Hallie: *I fed the one thing in my life that cares for me. Satisfied?*

Solace: *Far from it. But it'll do. Show me your bedroom.*

Hallie: *Lacking spank bank material?*

Solace: *That mouth will get you into trouble tomorrow, beautiful.*

The next message was a picture of the cat on a queen sized bed with plain white pillows and a gray and white coverlet.

Hallie: *That's all you get. Don't be pushy.*
    Solace: *I appreciate the gesture. And the pussy.*
    Hallie: 🖕

I laughed outright. The sound echoed across the empty parking lot.

Solace: I earned that. Goodnight, Hallie. I'll be in early tomorrow.
    Hallie: Goodnight Solace.
    Hallie: Thank you for following me. I did like it.

I closed my phone, grinning like a fucking idiot as I climbed into my car, lapping the city once before I headed home and showered in cold water. My hand stroked myself to a denied orgasm that left me sagging against the icy tiles in a hot mess as I thought of the girl who faced me despite her fear and didn't run.

Maybe she should have run. We'd see if she did tomorrow.

CHAPTER THREE

HALLIE

I avoided the training centre and the gym for the next week, and though I knew Solace followed me to the bus each night, he never walked beside me again after our heart shattering, panty-staining conversation.

Though each night I sent him a picture of my doormat, or my cat, or my slippers. And once, my bed.

And each night he replied the same way.

Solace: *Thank you, beautiful. I'll be in the gym early in the morning.*

No pressure, nothing. Somehow, weirdly, I felt more protected than ever.

Which left me back in the office, doing my job and being kind of...normal. Only I wasn't, because every time one of the team came in, I checked.

And not once, not one single time, did Solace enter the office in the last week. After touching me, the way he spoke, taunting, teasing...so much more than a simple water cooler flirtfest.

Or was it? Maybe this was his brand of flirting, and I bought too much into it. But I didn't think so. I doubted the other boys asked for shots of their casual fling's beds, or checked they got home. Maybe they did. I hadn't been part of enough healthy relationships to know.

All I did know was that Solace Hunter offered the best and worst distraction of my short lived career and if I didn't get my head out of the locker room, I wouldn't have one.

A head, or a career.

I stared at the green cells on my spreadsheet. I had no idea what the data set was meant to be or how long I'd been looking at it. The information merged the longer I tried to focus and couldn't. When I grabbed for my coffee not only was there a scant inch of liquid left in my oversized thermos, the whole lot had long gone cold.

A quick check on my screen told me it was past lunchtime. That's how long I'd stared fruitlessly at the screen pining over a muscular Chimera who I couldn't have anyway. Sighing, I pushed back from my desk and ignored the gaggle at the water cooler who had probably congregated there since their training session ended after morning tea. That was when the team's photoshoot for this week's media started, and the social gatherings across the office took off.

I'd become mostly immune to the comings and goings after my recent habitual Solace check, annoying as that had become. And it seemed that Janelle had indeed been inducted into team WAG sometime in the last week by the team's captain, Huxley Radfield, while I let myself be distracted by a certain defender of my own.

But he's not your own.

And I wasn't—nor would I ever be—his.

The thought was so ridiculous I couldn't even try to play with it. Solace had his pick of any woman he wanted. He could flirt, or whatever, all he liked with me but at the end of the day I was a barely graduated marketing nobody. An overweight, lonely girl who lived alone and ignored her cat too often.

And my last relationship with a hockey player ended disastrously. Thankfully that was a long time ago, and I never looked back.

Mooning over my cold coffee, I headed for the small staff kitchenette that doubled as the meeting place for pretty much everyone and squeezed into the corner that held the toaster, my crappy instant coffee, and my avocado collection. All three were fairly safe as the rest of the staff and hangers on who preferred the snob's version of coffee. While I could afford to drink it, I couldn't justify the cost on my meagre wage, and I knew bread wasn't an option for the majority of the WAGS.

So, my avocado collection was thankfully safe on all counts.

Humming away to myself, I buttered my bread, made my coffee with extra milk and sliced my avocado. In what was probably my third worst decision of the day, I slathered the whole thing onto my toast when I judged it had literally a few hours left of ultimate ripeness before it turned into that horrific state where dark spots appeared and then there would be no saving it.

A true tragedy.

My rescue strategy seemed a whole lot kinder, and I fully intended to enjoy my feast. I raised my toast to my mouth.

"You know how fattening those things are."

The toast stopped due to the proximity of the voice. I closed my eyes, still facing the corner and risked moving my toast closer to home.

"I mean, if you eat anything else, we'll have to put you somewhere in the back where you can't be seen."

Silence fell over the kitchen.

I opened my eyes, and swivelled around on my heel to find Janelle smirking at me and my avocado toast. Mindy glared at me over her shoulder. Apparently the promotion to team WAG hadn't done either of them any favours.

But that wasn't about to be Today Hallie's problem. I had no idea where the push came from. Maybe Solace's flirting gave me an extra confidence boost. Maybe it was insanity and a career death defying move. Who knew. I remembered how reckless I'd been standing before him outside the office building.

A grin crossed my face, born of the same kind of mad energy from that night. I pushed the *entire* quarter of toast that should have taken a whole lot longer to eat into my mouth, moaning and chewing loudly.

Really, over the top, food-porn loud.

Enough that they could have heard me in the training room. Maybe in the offices, too.

The WAGS mouths fell open as I chewed. I reached back blindly for the rest, getting avocado all over my hands, and stuffed that in, too.

"So good," I moaned, playing it right up and getting really, really messy.

Childish, such a bad idea, and I'd pay for it later not so subtly with these girls.

But by God was it worth it in that moment to see the shock on their faces.

More heads popped into the kitchen from the open doors at both ends. Faces I recognized as players from the team, and some of the sponsors. I gave someone—I didn't recognise who—a saucy wink as I managed to swallow, and that someone groaned.

I tossed my hair over my shoulders, and finished the whole show off by licking my fingers loudly in the utter silence that otherwise filled the area. With what felt like a hundred eyes locked on me, I turned to wash my hands. Heat crept up my cheeks as I realized what I'd just done, but now was not the time for shame. I refused flat out to wear someone else's insecurities.

I might not be dating a player, and I might not wear a flashy ring, but that didn't mean I had to put up with someone else's judgement about what I wore or how—or what—I ate at work.

Hell, tomorrow I could do the same again with melted chocolate. Normalize this shit.

My head held high, I turned back around ready to face the consequences of my actions and came face to chest with a seething hockey player, his heart beating loud and fast enough I could hear it from the outside.

Likely so could everyone else in the vicinity.

I raised my eyes to meet Solace's and he was *furious.*

Anger radiated from him as he glared down at me. Fists clenched and unclenched at his sides. A muscle ticked in his jaw as his thick, muscular thighs that were the stuff of legend the country round pressed mine back into the bench.

Three words made it past his bared teeth before he gripped my wrist in an unbreakable hold. "With me. *Now.*"

I might not have minded the way he gave orders before. I kind of didn't even mind how he stalked me in the parking lot in what became our personal evening ritual. Built this, right here? This was too far. Too much like staking a claim.

I couldn't do this. Not again.

"No. Nuh uh, Solace. Not a–"

Typical him, I never got a chance to finish that sentence. His grip solidified as he hauled me out of the kitchen so fast that I stopped talking just to concentrate on keeping my feet from tripping over each other. Mindy flipped me off as I sailed past her.

I had no recourse but to follow Solace as he yanked me along behind him down the hall, trying locked doors. He snapped up a lanyard with a swipe key from a hook and turned down a corridor, trying the next office. That one gave.

Solace pushed the door open, towing me inside. I stumbled across the threshold, turning on him as he shut the door gently and locked us in.

"What the hell was that?" I started, storming forward. "You can't just—"

"Me? The hell did you think *you* were doing?" He turned back to face me.

I faltered at the undisguised lust written across his face aimed right at me, so close. Because my little tantrum reduced the space between us and brought me within arm's reach of the Chimeras' defender which seemed suddenly like a really bad, bad decision.

"Solace," I whispered, back pedalling.

But my chance to escape him faded as he took up the offensive, stalking toward me. One arm latched around my waist, pulling me into his body even as he continued to pace forward, propelling me backward. The other swept out behind me and cleared everything off the sponsor's desk.

"You can't do that—" I objected.

"Those noises you made in that room belong to me," he hissed in my face.

In a single breath he lifted me off the ground and planted my ass on the corner of the desk so my legs parted. He leaned over me until I scrambled backward but since he refused to let me go the only place I could go was downward. Cowering.

This is so bad.

Breath evacuated from me as I scraped at the desk with one hand, the other knotting in his shirt. "Solace, stop. This isn't a good—"

"The only sounds I want to hear out of you right now are either more of what you did in the kitchen, only just for me this time, or begging me to fuck you," he snapped, releasing me with one hand to rake his fingers through his hair.

I stared at him, my mouth open as my heart slammed into my ribcage and–stopped.

"What?"

"Make those fucking moans for me, Hallie." His voice softened a touch. "Do that for me, and I'll find out how well we fit on this damn desk together."

Swallowing on a dry throat was another bad idea but my brain jammed, and nothing seemed to make it through. "You can't be serious," I murmured, choking on a disparaging laugh. "This is *me*, Solace. I'm not one of the girls out there."

"I don't want them. I want you." He glared into my eyes as though his desire was my personal fault.

I shook my head. "You're insane. No one wants me."

"Stop it." His grip tightened as he ground his groin into me, and there was plenty of evidence right there. "I fucking want you. Hell, girl. I can barely sleep for wanting you. The earlier you get here, the earlier I have to arrive each morning to know you're safe on your own. Same at night. Shit, I've considered following you home just to wait outside your window and see your lights go on and off. Sleep in the car, maybe." He panted a little, his enormous palms dwarfing my arms where he squeezed me rhythmically as he spoke.

"Wait, you're serious?" I whispered. "Solace— I don't have a good dating history. Especially with hockey players."

"So you just want to fuck, then?" His growl ripped through me.

I shook my head, flinging my hair around my face. "No. *No.* I'm not doing casual with you. I— I can't do that."

I tore my gaze away, unwilling to read the disappointment in his face. Unable to believe I just said that. This was *Solace Hunter.* For fuck's sake, if there was anyone in my life to fuck around with, it was this man.

"Good. I don't want that either." His breath came heavy on my neck. "But I'm still going to fuck you."

"What?" I gripped his shoulders, barely able to close my fingers around some of the muscle there. "Dammit. You're too big."

He laughed, the sound low and dark. "Oh, beautiful. You have no idea." His hand covered mine as he shoved my palm between us and closed it around his erection straining through his jeans.

I couldn't grasp him there any more than I could his shoulders.

My whimper filled the room as the scent of my arousal drifted between us. "Baby Jesus."

His smile bordered on cruel, and it set off something twisted inside me. "There's that sound I wanted to hear." His hands skated along my thighs, squeezing hard enough to bruise, digging his fingers into my flesh beneath. "Fuck what they all want or look like, Hallie. I need a girl who's soft and plump beneath me. Someone I can sink into. Someone who hears me *here.*" Solace tapped my forehead. "I don't need someone hard. That's my damn job, you understand?"

Unyielding eyes glinted, almost maniacal as I lost myself in him, leaning back when he pushed me down onto the desk.

"I understand," I whispered.

"Good." He traced the seams on the insides of my purple tights beneath my short, black skirt. "I like these."

"I like them too," I admitted.

"Then I'll buy you more." His hand gripped right over my pussy and ripped hard.

The tearing sound barely covered the yelp that tore from me, but it didn't matter. His mouth slammed over mine, swallowing my small scream as his fingers found bare flesh and pushed inside.

I screamed again as he fingered me brutally. Solace swallowed those noises too, his tongue echoing the motion between my legs. He was every-where, arched over me, filling my mouth and my pussy. Thick fingers, thick tongue, bruising, leaving me aching for more of him.

Barely able to breathe, I twisted beneath him but he refused to let me up. My hips bucked against the heel of his hand that rubbed my clit. The world whitened out within seconds as my breath stuttered, and his free hand caught the back of my head before it thumped onto the desktop.

"Christ, Hallie. So wet and tight." The manic light never left his dark eyes as he came back into focus. "I can't wait to stretch that pretty little pussy out."

I whimpered as he played between my legs, each movement making a horrific sloshing sound that drew heat from my nipples to my cheeks and somehow managed to increase my arousal rather than dampen it.

"This is— we—" I gasped sentence fragments, my legs shaking.

"Tonight I'll stay late. In the gym," Solace panted above me, rubbing himself against my body. "You'll wear these tights wet and open like this for the rest of the day. I want you to think about how drenched you are right now, the sorts of noises you're making for me. When your work is finished, and you can't stand it anymore, I want you to come and find me. Then we can do something about this." He withdrew his fingers and tapped my pussy once, twice. I screamed softly as the wet sound reverberated around us. "Do you understand?" His mouth crashed against mine before I could answer.

I nodded frantically through his kiss. "I understand, Solace."

"Good girl," he breathed, trailing kisses along my jaw as he toyed gently between my legs like I was his personal playground. "So beautiful. Fuck, I can't wait to see all of you bare for me."

A low moan filled the space between us and it took a moment before I figured out it came from me.

Solace closed his eyes, sucking in a shuddering breath. "Do that again and I'll fuck you right now," he murmured, squeezing my thighs with wet fingers.

I stilled, trying to close my hands around his wrists, and failed. He nodded, seeming to get himself under control, and pulled me back up.

"You gonna be all right for the rest of the day?" HIs lips touched the corner of mine in a barely there kiss I struggled to associate with the man who just tore me a new one–literally.

"I think I like it when you're gentler," I confessed, tugging my skirt down and avoiding his eyes.

His knuckles caught beneath my chin, forcing my face to his. Reluctantly, I met his gaze, losing myself in those charcoal eyes instantly.

"As long as you keep that sort of behavior between just us from now on, I'll stay gentle with you. But moan like that where my boys can hear?" His hand wrapped around my nape, dragging me closer. "Beautiful, I've got limits. I don't share, and you're mine."

I struggled to breathe. "You don't have a claim on me." The room shrank to just us, too tight.

I can't do this again.

It's different this time.

I closed my eyes, squeezed them shut tight.

"Look at me, Hallie," he ordered.

I took a full breath in and out while he massaged the back of my neck before I managed to open my eyes, shocked when they filled with tears. "I can't do this again."

"Tell me." The same order, but gentler this time.

He had promised.

"I—" I bit my lip, starting without meaning to let the words out. I'd never told anyone else what happened with Travis. Just let the media believe we fell apart for all the reasons a girl like me didn't suit a pro hockey player. "He liked puck bunnies," I whispered. "After games when I–he'd send me home. And I–" I swallowed, refusing to cry for a heart broken long ago. "I've never been one of them."

Solace's face hardened. "He cheated on you?"

I nodded, but the hurt there was still so raw, even after three years. "Yes," I said unsteadily, and looked down.

He let me, folding his arms around my body and pulled me in close. "You need to cry?"

I sniffled. "No."

"Liar." I could hear the smile in his voice before it changed. "You ever cry?"

"Too many nights."

"Not anymore. Cry now if you need. After tonight you stay with me. If you cry after that, then it's for a different reason." His lips grazed my ear. "I can teach you pleasure in denial and I can make you cry, beautiful. Want me to teach you that?"

A frisson of need rippled over my skin. "I'm so out of my depth," I whispered, shocked my nipples hardened at his filthy words.

Solace laughed, cupping my breast and squeezing gently as though he already knew my body's reaction. "Let me teach you everything." He kissed my temple. "Let me show you what it's supposed to be like."

I risked looking up at him, unsure if his promises would give me all that he offered...or if he'd break me.

Dark eyes stared down into mine, unflinching.

This was the man who followed me each night for months. Who tried to scare me and made sure I got home safely. Who protected me and wanted me above everything else.

Who might be worth the risk.

Worrying my bottom lip between my teeth, I nodded once, and prayed I wasn't making a mistake.

"All right," I breathed, hating the way my voice broke, hating how I trembled in his arms.

Though he seemed to love that from the way his hands tightened on me.

"Tonight."

CHAPTER FOUR

SOLACE

A word in Cap's ear, and the vultures stayed the fuck away from my girl. Damn, for a moment there I thought she'd been scared off. Who the hell ever hurt her did a damn fine job but I got it—the same reason she couldn't trust anyone and lived alone was the same reason I didn't play with the puck bunnies or join team WAGS.

Staying out of Hallie's way all day and not haunting her every step was my next challenge. I managed to watch her occasionally, especially when the media crew turned up for the afternoon shoot. Keeping an eye on the door I posed with the rest of the team, but I never got the chance to head into the office any more than I had the last week since I finally approached her.

Between training and promotions during the season I barely had time to think. The rest of the team might spend their evenings socialising and living it up, but the culture never sat well with me. We signed on to do a job, so that's what I did.

Someone spritzed oil on my back and rubbed it in massage style, but I threw the hands off. I already hated this part, but I didn't need anyone touching me after what I just promised to Hallie.

"I got it," someone else muttered. Hands that weren't half as soft slapped my back hard.

I grunted at the intrusion but the contract wasn't unwelcome. "Thanks, man."

"Don't mention it." Shannon Incarsen, the player who noticed my distraction during training earlier in the week and capitalized on it, squeezed my shoulder hard. "Hux said you had trouble with the slut squad."

A snort left me. "Too apt, man."

His next squeeze wasn't so gentle. "My wife is counted as one of those."

I stilled, knowing the rough time he'd had with her. "Apologies, man."

"Don't mention it. I get it." He worked the oil in a

little longer than necessary as the rest of the shoot went on without us. "We had some shit years, Lori and me. But we came through. Never really let her go, you know. Mighta been wrong but...I couldn't give her up."

I grinned. "I know how that feels. Been watching Hallie for a while."

"Yeah? She the right one for you?"

I shrugged. "For me? Yeah. Me for her? Dunno yet. Guess we'll find out."

He laughed. "That's sweet, brother. I don't think I gave my girl a choice. She just had to come around to me."

"Sounds like an obsession."

"What we did... It didn't define healthy." He slapped my back head enough to leave a mark, and wandered away, talking loudly.

I rocked back onto my heels, thinking over what he'd said. Maybe I'd approached Hallie wrong. I knew she was it for me. Had known what I felt for her was more than lust for months even though we hadn't fucked yet.

She was my obsession. I couldn't think straight without her. Knowing that she knew I'd been there all that time did something to me. That she sat at the desk, working her ass off as always, her thighs smeared with the evidence of our frenzied playtime earlier and the gaping hole where I tore straight through her tights and her panties clean off...

Fuck, I had to stop thinking about her, or this photoshoot would have evidence of my own obsession and a damn fine boner to boot.

Forcing a smile I fucking hated, I pushed up to the balls of my feet under the guise of stretching, and let Hallie slide to the shadowy parts of my mind for later tonight.

I wasn't sure I'd be able to hold to my promise to be gentle with her after all.

Sweat rolled along my spine as I pushed the bar up for the dozenth time this rep plus some. I'd stopped counting minutes before. My eyes barely left the door, and my arms shook. Before that, it was my legs that trembled, though they weren't on the roster to work. Coach would be pissed I went off the schedule, but I didn't care.

I couldn't get Hallie off my mind but if she didn't haul her curvy ass through that door soon I'd either do it for her or storm into the office, flip her over her desk, and then all bets on being *gentle* were off.

My fingers cramped on the bar. I released the warmed metal, letting the bar up in a controlled raise as her shadow appeared in the doorway.

I closed my eyes. "Thank fuck," I muttered, soft enough my voice shouldn't have carried.

"Hey," Hallie said, walking toward me with short steps. "I wasn't sure if, you know, you changed your mind..." She stared at my sweating body and heaving chest with a furrowed brow. "Are you okay?"

I grinned and held out one hand, grabbing a water bottle with the other. "Yeah. I'm good. Stress relief. Wasn't sure you'd be here either."

More frowns. I decided I hated them on her. "You get those?" she asked, incredulous. "Really? Fear that I wouldn't turn up? Are you serious?"

I straightened and something in my back protested. I'd pay for the lack of stretching tomorrow, but right now all I cared about was the girl in front of me. "Hell yes, I'm scared shitless of rejection, beautiful."

"Someone like you?" She stared at me sceptically. "I find that hard to believe." Her arms folded beneath her breasts, pushing them up.

I swallowed hard. "Come here." I patted my knee, spreading my legs apart.

"You're sweaty. And filthy."

"And you're about to be." She'd have to get used to that. I didn't fuck cleanly.

Hallie hesitated, but she was here, and we had a deal. She walked through those damn doors tonight. I wasn't about to let her renege, not after the way she coated my hand with her slick juices back in the offices earlier.

Hell, I'd barely been able to hold my shit together in front of everyone when I heard those sultry moans that I *knew* came from her soft lips before I saw her little display in the kitchen. Then, the food show. Christ, the girl should be locked away. Preferably in my bedroom.

The way she sounded, the effect she had on everyone in that room... and she *had no fucking idea how hot she was*. More than one guy on my team nearly embarrassed himself when she swallowed. I nearly ripped someone's hand off when it strayed to his cock over his pants.

Which was the same reason I dragged her out of the room, and how we ended up here with her wearing ripped tights, her thighs painted in her own cum all day, and no one else the wiser.

But she wasn't coming any closer, and I still had some work to do in breaking down the walls between us.

"How was your day?" I asked the loaded question softly. My eyes flicked to the hem of her short skirt that she habitually wore over her tights that usually concealed everything. Thanks to our playtime earlier, today that same pretty hemline left her exposed.

Her hands travelled to her sides where she gripped the material under my heavy gaze and tugged it south. "Everyone left me alone," she said, confusion lifting her tone. "I– I thought after the kitchen there would be more, you know…"

"Bullying?" I kept my voice low, turning one hand up on my knee and curling my fingers inward.

She took an involuntary, jerky step toward me and halted. "Yes."

A smile curved my lips. "I know."

Hallie blinked. "You…did that?" She was afraid, and I hated it. "Don't do that."

"Don't protect you?" I raised my eyebrows. "I thought you liked me stalking you, beautiful. Now get that ass on my lap before I rip a different hole in those tights and find out what colour your skin turns when I spank you."

I didn't have to guess on that last; her cheeks stained the perfect shade of heat that shot blood straight to my cock.

"Stop being dirty." She surprised me when she strode forward, right up to me, her chin lifted in a show of defiance that floored me.

Better, when she lifted one curved thigh and straddled my waist, flashing me her still swollen pussy before she settled above me, not quite allowing our bodies to touch.

"Who are you?" I settled my hands on her waist, keeping my touch gentle though I wanted to squeeze and plump her body, haul her into me and kiss her until she creamed all over the front of my gym shorts. Fuck, I wanted her scent rubbed all over me so it'd never wash off. "Show me these tits," I ordered, sliding a hand over the swell of her stomach to grip the front of her shirt. "Show me what's mine."

Hallie batted my hand away with a derisive laugh. "Nothing on my body is yours, Solace. I'm my own person, and *if* I let you play with me, then you'll be grateful." Her hands drifted over mine, her sweet touch so at odds with her words that I couldn't breathe as she pulled her stretchy top down to expose her breasts to me.

Air stalled in my throat as I stared at her in awe, this stunning goddess straddling my lap, telling me I could only have her if she said so.

Fuck, I'd be on my knees, begging in a second if she denied me.

My cock strained to reach her heat as she rose above me, leaning forward until those gorgeous breasts were in my face.

"Lick," she murmured.

Given all the permission I needed, I cupped my hands around her offerings reverently, leaning forward and traced my tongue around her areola. The soft hiss of her breath brushed my temple as I laved her nipple, playing with her other breast as I cradled her in my arms. Keeping her safe and giving her pleasure became my dual focus. Nothing else mattered as I worshipped her.

Slowly, the tension I hadn't realized she carried released from her body as she sank down onto me. I welcomed the wet heat of her that dripped onto my cock. Reaching a hand between us, I shoved my shorts down, needing the skin-on-skin contact. When she struggled in my arms I broke back from my attention to her nipples.

"I need to feel you over me," I said hoarsely. "Nothing else yet, beautiful. Let me have this. Please."

She nodded at whatever she saw in my face, pressing her body down onto mine. I groaned aloud, letting my eyes fall shut at the glorious pleasure of having her body contact mine. It wasn't complete yet; we still had clothes in the way. But damn, it was a close thing.

"Better?" she asked kind of innocently, though I swore she held back some of her sass that laced her tone.

I reached behind her, ripped those tights as promised, and spanked that ass hard. "I warned you, beautiful."

She yelped, crashing forward into me. Shock reflected on her pretty face as I held her to me, rubbing circles over the flesh I just tortured. "Why did you—"

"No one ever spank you before, huh?" I mused, my cock thickening against her swollen pussy lips. I needed to be inside her *now*.

She shook her head, her bottom lip trembling a little. "No. I don't understand you," she whispered, a little wildly. A plethora of emotions scrolled across her face, the overwhelm too much for her to manage.

I stopped my petting, and cupped her face. "Breathe," I commanded, playing the pads of my thumbs over her swollen mouth. "Nice and deep. Be good for me, then I'll kiss you. Then you're gonna come for me, nice and slow, and when you come down, soaking my dick, you're gonna take all of me. Okay, beautiful?"

She nodded, her gaze unfocused as I leaned forward and brushed my mouth over hers. "Breathe, Hallie," I whispered, waiting long enough for her to take a single, deep inhale before I fused our mouths together, gliding my tongue along hers.

Her tiny sounds, those whimpers and whines I thought I craved had *nothing* on the way she rubbed her sopping pussy over my length as she kissed me back. I groaned into her mouth, cupping the back of her head and kissed her harder, needing her lips as swollen as the ones that curled around my cock.

"Please," she whimpered against my mouth. "I need to–" She choked up.

Heat returned to her cheeks under my hands, but the need reflected in her eyes told me everything I needed to know.

"You wanna come?" I cupped the back of her neck, holding her in place. A streak of my cruelty fired up as she writhed on my lap, needy as fuck. "Right here in the gym, with your clothes torn open so and your tits out so anyone who walks through that door can see you?"

Not that anyone was around or would *be* around

because they fucking well knew better than to turn up tonight on pain of eating their own castration by my hand. Every motherfucker on the team knew to stay well away. But Hallie didn't know what I threatened, and that suited me just fine. My other hand closed around her nipple, tweaking gently, milking her.

Her eyes widened, panic shutting off her brain as her body responded to the tease I set up. That pretty pussy massaging my cock gushed nice and hot for me.

"Solace, I can't lose my job," she gasped, twisting in my hold, but there was nowhere for her to go.

No way I was letting her up, not now.

"Imagine what the guys will smell when they come in to work out tomorrow. Your pussy juices all over the machine, heady as fuck. Think they'd recognize it from the office? I know how turned on you were all day," I murmured against her mouth, pressing a hand to her ass and gliding her along my cock.

Her moan nearly undid me on the spot. I cramped my foot purposefully, using the pain to draw back on my own need. Denial was the game, right? Edge and pull back. Edge both of us again.

When we came together, we would be fucking explosive.

"How do you know," she gasped, rocking with me, the sounds of her arousal sucking along my drenched cock. "I looked for you all day. You weren't —" Tears sprang to her eyes as she stared at me in utter desperation. "You weren't *there*."

My hand tightened on the back of her neck bringing her impossibly closer. *She looked for me.*

"I was there, watching you, little office girl. I made sure all your things were in the kitchen between training rounds and shoots. I made sure the doors were locked after everyone left. I made sure you had enough coffee and time to work while I thrashed myself fucking stupid in here and didn't bend you over your desk and fuck you into oblivion before you were ready. I made it *your choice* to come to me tonight. Fuck, I made sure no one else would be here to see you," I growled, my voice cracking on my final confession.

So much for not telling her.

Her eyes widened in surprise, or maybe it was something else. Those thighs clamped about me, trembling as she came hard. A soft noise I hadn't heard from her before elicited from her lips as she tipped her head back. Every part of her softened.

Heat soaked my cock as I held her trembling body against me when she couldn't hold herself up.

"Fuck, that was beautiful." I stared at her, a lump forming in my throat I could barely speak around. "Jesus, I love you."

Her fingers shook on my shoulders where they curled for purchase, slipping on my sweat beaded skin. "You can't say that," she whispered, her voice a bare thread as her head tipped forward.

I cradled her into my shoulder, lifting her hips and ignored that last. "I'm going to fuck you now," I said gently, positioning my cock at her entrance, easing the head into her tight, flooded pussy.

Her whine grew as I pushed in, nails clawing against my chest. "Solace, I can't–"

"You can," I murmured, stroking her neck. She curled into me, but I held her back a little, needing to see her face. "Am I hurting you?"

"N– No, the pressure is a lot," she whimpered, wiggling her hips and managed to take another inch of me.

I groaned, and clamped my hands to her waist. "Fuck me, beautiful. I'll last less than ten seconds if you do that."

She raised her head, a sassy look in her eye that I'd come to associate with her brand of defiance.

"Yeah?" She panted, straightening and pressed her hands to my shoulders. "So I'm in control if I do..." She pushed down, her thighs squeezing my hips as she took my length almost in one.

I gritted my teeth, holding her gaze. "Fuck, beautiful. That's a sight I'll never forget."

Or a feeling. My balls tried to draw up, but I cramped a leg and flexed my foot, drawing back from the edge fast. When I could get a breath in, Hallie's perfectly plump ass pressed to my balls, and she moaned, her pussy strangling my cock deep and tight.

She stared at me, her thighs trembling and I knew she'd reached her limit. Hell, I was close to mine.

Cupping her hips gently, I squeezed and lifted her easily, sliding her up my length and bringing her down again, testing the feel of her, how she took me. Small whines grew from her lips as I increased the pace.

"Going okay?" I asked, finding her mouth with mine in a sweet kiss that brought me back to the edge when her tongue toyed sensually with mine.

Christ, this girl... When I told her I loved her it was no line. I'd followed her for weeks, thought about nothing but her. She was in my fucking blood.

I knew I'd had my eye on her for longer than she thought of me, and I was good to wait, if that's what she needed. But I never said I'd be fair about it.

If giving her orgasms, spoiling her, and stalking her at work meant earning brownie points for my case, I'd do what it took to make her fall for me, too.

She moaned loud into my mouth, and I was done.

My fingers sank into her beautiful flesh as I drove her onto my cock, shoving my hips up at an increasing pace, railing her from below. Pants burst from her, cries ripped from her swollen lips that I licked and let her scream for me.

Her short nails sank into my shoulders as I fucked her, ruining her as she marked me. Promo shots might have to be with a shirt on for a while. I didn't care. Her tits were back in my face. I caught a nipple with my teeth, sucking and licking until her pussy contracted, then bit down lightly.

Hallie detonated on me, creaming on my cock like it was her favourite sort of eclair. Her scream reverberated around the gym, and I knew every time I walked into this room I'd hear that sound. She rode me through her orgasm, running that one into the next. Those thighs never stopped trembling as I pounded her from below, finally releasing my hold on my own pleasure.

Her name met her screams as I roared, tipping my head back and filled her to overflowing. Those thighs clamped around me as she sank her pretty lips to my shoulders, sobbing and trembling and moaning.

My heart slammed into my ribcage as I threaded my hands through her hair and cradled her spent form to my body. It took more than one try to stand before I could carry her to the showers on trembling legs of my own. As much as I wanted to make her walk out of here with my cum trailing down the insides of her edible thighs, I had better plans for cleaning her up, starting with my tongue.

CHAPTER FIVE

HALLIE

A handful of days after Solace took me to the bus—I wouldn't let him take me home—from our night in the gym, I swore my legs still shook whenever he walked into the office. Or the kitchen, or whatever room I was in at the time. His looks never changed, always watching, always careful, unless we were alone. Then they grew heated and, well, so did everything else.

Not that we hid anything—the team and WAGS and office knew something was going on between us —because he seemed to gravitate toward me, or just plain stalked me every time I moved. But he never touched me or kissed me in plain view out of respect of my plea not to jeopardize the job I still wasn't sure if I loved or hated, except that it allowed me more time near him.

Nor had I forgotten that he told me he loved me that night, though he hadn't said anything similar since. I appreciated that...maybe. Solace's silence confused the shit out of me. As always, no pressure, a respectful distance while I made up my own mind. Until we were together—then he was the filthiest, dirtiest player out there.

Forcing my thoughts back to my work for the day I topped up my coffee in the kitchen, all too aware he leaned against the wall opposite, shrinking the small room.

"You gonna come home with me tonight, beautiful?" he asked in a low voice.

I checked over my shoulder to ensure that we were alone, but no one else socialized around us, for once. A rare moment. I unscrewed and rescrewed the top of my coffee thermos for something to do.

He offered the same thing every night since we had sex in the gym, but I hadn't had the courage to say yes to him yet. The disappointment on his face that night had been brief, but it was there when I asked him to take me to the bus in a voice that wouldn't stop shaking. I wasn't sure if I was going to cry or explode, but everything with him, as per usual, was so big and huge and overwhelming.

I needed time to myself and I wasn't ready to capitalize on whatever this was fast becoming. Because I'd been here before and my heart broke. So yeah, I was scared it would happen again.

Same environment, same puck bunnies in attendance.

Or at least, close enough.

"I thought we didn't do this at work?" I murmured, stalling for time with the top of my thermos again.

Solace detached himself from the wall in my periphery and stalked closer. His enormous, inked hand closed over mine. "You'll break it if you do that, you know," he murmured. "And then I'll owe you more than a dozen pairs of your favourite tights."

I blinked up at him. "Why do I need a dozen?"

His smile was downright sinful. "So I can destroy them whenever the fuck I want, beautiful."

His fingertips grazed my cheek before he cupped the back of my neck, massaging there firmly, keeping his touch gentle. I loved that about him, that he knew not to scare me when I asked him not to, but that he seemed to know when to push that boundary for both of us.

The sex was incredible. Life rending. Amazing. After him, there would be no one else. I knew that. Yet I couldn't bring myself to believe that he wouldn't be like the last player who toyed with my heart so freely.

"We weren't doing this at work, remember?" I said softly, tilting my head back, though I didn't quite pull away, letting a warning tone slide into my voice.

Solace nodded, though he didn't stop. Nor did I expect him to, really. "I remember. I also remember telling you I loved you, and that you're mine." His tone held a fierce edge to it, engaging a battle of wills in a quiet space.

My heart stopped for a fraction of a second then restarted. I coughed a little and he took the opportunity to draw me closer, liberating my thermos and catching both my hands in one of his.

"Please, not here," I begged.

His eyes darkened. "Tonight, and I'll make you beg for something else."

Before I could stop him, his head dipped and his mouth covered mine in a deep kiss that left me shaking on my feet.

"You shouldn't—"

"I don't want to not have you when I want," he muttered against my mouth.

I shook my head, my curls hitting my cheeks. "I'm not your toy, Solace," I whispered back.

"But I want to play with you," he countered.

My heart shattered in my chest. I tugged my wrists free of his hold and miraculously, he let me go. "Toys get replaced. Set aside. I've been the toy that was left. You know that." I turned my head away, horrified when my vision blurred.

His hand at my neck turned my head back. Damnit, I couldn't escape him at all. "You're not who I'll ever be bored of Hallie. I promise." His dark eyes bored into mine, and I so desperately wanted to believe him.

"What if you just don't know yet?" I couldn't take that heartbreak again. I knew I couldn't. "The last time... it hurt so bad." I couldn't believe I was saying this to anyone, let alone him.

A cough at his back stiffened his body. "What do you want?"

"Just the coffee, Solace," a sugary sweet voice I knew *that I knew* too well floated over us like a cloud of sticky cotton candy.

I broke back from Solace with a gasp to find two gold talons curled into his bicep.

She can get her fingers around his shoulder better than I can.

My rational thought was obliterated as I found his eyes, the discontent there. He shrugged her hand off, his mouth turned down.

"This is my girl's coffee. The other stuff's over there," Solace dismissed her without another look.

It can't be. Don't check.

But I had to, peeking about his shoulder. Kylie Smart, the same OW in my relationship with Travis smiled back at me, baring fangs I swore had been sharpened since the last time I saw her years ago. Somehow her body looked more toned, more golden. Even her hair was blonder. The line of her jaw stood out as more angular.

I had no idea how that was possible, but the girl who gave me so much grief and cost me a broken heart as well as a broken relationship stood in the same damn room as me, and just had her claws in my man.

My man.

I shouldn't have looked.

"Hallie," Solace murmured. Concern and authority laced his voice. "Talk to me."

I shook my head, pushing at his chest then his shoulder when he wouldn't budge. "Let me out."

He sighed and stepped back, his fingers trailing my wrist. "Tonight?"

I shook my head, kept my eyes on my floor and scurried back to my desk, setting up my work for the afternoon behind a towering in tray that thankfully allowed me to hide from everyone else. Kylie didn't approach me. I called that a win, but then the doubts crept in. *I walked away from Solace. She had her hands on him.* The familiar tendrils of panic latched into my heart, all too ready in shred mode as I sat frozen at my desk, and didn't leave.

I hid. Because I couldn't see that, not again.

Solace didn't approach me for the rest of the day. I wasn't sure if that was a good thing or a bad thing. Nor did I see him when I headed for my bus, my single footsteps my only company for once.

When I got home to my cat, Mica, my hands shook so much I could barely feed her. Shaking and crying stupidly over something that happened so long ago. Something I thought I'd managed to extricate myself from.

Stumbling into my room without turning on a single light, I sat on my bed, thumbing through my phone. Travis's number sat right below Solace's. I held my breath as I ran the pad of my finger over the screen. Calling him would be ludicrous. We didn't part on good terms, and calling him now would look like begging.

Shaking my head I tossed my phone onto my bedside table, then remembered to charge it. I yanked my clothes off over my head, slipped into bed without eating to Mica's greatest disgrace, and tried to fall asleep.

Sometime after midnight, I half woke from a dose of a half-dream, half horrendous nightmarish memory about a puck bunny in a pink dress and gold nails wrapped around Solace to realise I hadn't sent him a message to say I'd gotten home safely. I rolled over, knocking Mica off the bed. She mewled piteously and leapt off the mattress. Her feet pattered across my floor as she slipped out of the bedroom door to find somewhere else to sleep for the rest of the night, leaving me alone and feeling more guilty than ever.

I flicked the screen on my phone and nearly blinded myself. Two AM. It was way too late for me to message a man and risk waking him. Especially someone like Solace who went home the last thing at night and got up hellishly early to be there when I opened the office too. I couldn't wake him now, if he even cared after the way I blew him off.

Fresh tears tracked my cheeks, the overwhelm of

the whole week leaving me shuddering and alone through the coldest hours of the night. I pressed my cheek to the cold pillow, and tried not to remember the night that the last hockey player brought home a puck bunny to the bed we shared because he'd been drunk enough to forget I lived there too.

I opened my door the next morning—well, the same morning, really—grumpy, tired and bitching about leaving my thermos in the Chimera's kitchen. I was *still* muttering about it while pushing Mica's head back in the door so she didn't escape and so distracted that I nearly screamed at the behemoth standing right on my freaking doorstep.

"Holy shit, Solace." I thwacked him with the back of my free hand and hurt myself. That earned him another glare that he fully deserved. "What are you doing here?"

"I thought you said you weren't a screamer." He surveyed me with a tired smile, though his eyes travelled over my body hungrily. *No change there.* His rumpled clothes were, though. "No tights today, huh?"

I cocked a hip, pleased when Mica's fluffy head

finally squished back in where it should be, and my door locked. "Someone wrecked my best ones."

He braced an arm over my head, pushing my freshly filled coffee thermos into my hands. "I promised you I'd get you more." His eyes searched mine.

I swallowed and stared back, unsure what this was exactly as I spotted his yellow sports coupe parked right out front of my rental townhouse. "Thank you for getting me coffee." Then my mind thunked into place without its usual caffeinated morning lubricant. "Wait, have you been out here all night?"

He shrugged. "I wanted to make sure you got home alright."

I gaped at him guppie style. "I woke up at two in the morning and felt so guilty. If I'd known, I would have—" I closed my mouth with a snap.

His eyes glittered at me. "Hallie, are you telling me I should have been camping out here all week rather than pining for you at home and edging fuck out of myself when I couldn't have you, beautiful?" The predator in him rose to full heat.

I backed into my door, flattening myself to the scarred wood, but there was no way around him.

"Solace, you're too much, sometimes," I murmured, my breaths coming short.

"Only sometimes, huh?" He caught my chin with his knuckles and grazed his mouth over mine. "Did you eat last night?" That came out as a demand.

I bit my lip and shook my head. "No."

He nodded. "I didn't think so. I watched you go inside, and the place stayed dark. My heart fucking shattered, Hallie. I came so close to pounding on that door until you answered, but I didn't wanna scare you."

My vision of him blurred. "I wish you had."

"Christ." His arms dropped, folding around me and my thermos. Mica pawed and mewled at the door from the other side frantically. "Hell, I'm scaring your other pussy."

I giggled in his arms, resting my head against his chest. The rhythmic beat of his heat, strong and slow, settled me as I breathed at the same rate. My arms tightened around him. "I'm sorry. You shouldn't have slept rough because of me."

"But I did." He tangled his fingers through my hair, massaging my scalp. "You know why."

I nodded, knowing what he'd say and weirdly, I didn't need to hear it anymore. I'd kind of come to accept who he was and how we were in the last hours, though my heart still bore the scars another man left in the same place.

"This is scary to me," I whispered. "It hurt so much last time."

"Not gonna happen," he said firmly, crushing me to him.

"Coffee cup," I choked out, managing a breath when he released me.

"Sorry," he said sheepishly, pulling my clothes right. "Have we got time to get you some breakfast before we go in?"

I stared at him, my mouth falling open. "But you have training this morning. Then practice. And a commercial that films at nine."

He grinned at me. "Beautiful, you know my schedule better than I do."

I shrugged. "I kind of know the whole team's schedule. It's my job."

He frowned, and I hurried to remove it from his face, smoothing the deep lines with my fingers.

"No, it's not that I don't stalk *your* schedule. I do... Actually, I always have. And your stats. You know, when you beat Newtown? That was your best game of the season. We were trounced. Seventeen saves, Solace. That put you at a .937, you know that? I mean you guys were coming off a buck's night, and

Coach was furious, but whatever. It made you top of the league, saves percentage wise. You still can't be beat." I stopped rambling when he stared at me, bemused. "What?"

"Why aren't you my PA? Or on our management team? Why are you wasted running over whatever the fuck you do hiding behind paperwork all day long?" His soft voice rocked my world on its axis.

I nibbled my lip. "You really mean it, don't you?"

He didn't have to ask what I meant, knowing I wasn't talking about work. "Yeah, Hallie. I do."

My eyes shuttered as I sucked in a long breath. "Okay. Let's try this thing."

"Yeah?" The way his voice lifted left me grinning.

I pushed his shoulder with my thermos. "Break-fast, Solace. I'm talking about breakfast."

His laugh stayed with me all the way to his car, his hand wrapped around mine. In the end we got drive through with sparkling tea and egg and bacon wraps that I drooled all over, knowing it wasn't part of his nutritional chart.

Solace threw the whole schedule out the window literally, driving us to the Point that overlooked the bay and the ships coming around the top of the headland.

His arm slung around my shoulder, we ate in

relative silence, me snuggled into him, picking cat fur off my bottle green skirt when I ran out of things to do with my hands. After a while he sighed and covered my fingers with his, stopping my incessant picking.

"You know, I have to take you shopping," he said in a tight voice.

"Why?" I frowned at him and down at my skirt. "I like this one."

"Yeah, so do I," he said ruefully. "But if I have to watch the team stare at your bare legs today, I'm not gonna be much of a defender for them, beautiful. Just you." He kissed the tip of my nose, then my cheeks and finally my mouth, long and slow and deep, laying the seat back until his body covered mine and his hand slid beneath my skirt.

I moaned softly into his mouth, digging my nails into his arms. "We need to get to work," I murmured, gasping as he flicked my panties aside.

"Yeah, in a bit." He frowned down at me. "I spent the whole fucking night in this car, you know," he said slowly, running his fingers through my pussy lips, collecting the copious amount of moisture there. "Worrying about you." He kissed me hard. "Desperate for you." Another kiss. "All I wanted was to fold you in my arms, kiss the shit out of you, and know you were safe. Mine," he growled, a taste of his darkness descending over his eyes.

I opened my mouth to object that his discomfort wasn't *all* my fault, but that was as far as I got.

Two thick fingers speared straight inside me, working fast and hard. Fluid coated the insides of my thighs as I cried out into his mouth that crushed mine. My hips bucked up. I arched, knowing I'd come for him in less than a seco—

His hand withdrew and he gripped the inside of my thigh painfully, pulling the tender flesh up. Then he released his grip and smacked me with an open palm. The sound ricocheted around the inside of his car.

"Don't you leave me wanting you like that. Scared for you. Fuck, beautiful," he muttered dangerously. "I spent the night with a broken heart, not sure you'd want me again."

"Me too," I whispered, wincing when he slapped the inside of my other thigh, spotting how far down his finger marks would be. "Whoa, stop," I panicked. "They'll see."

"No," he ground out. "I fucking well won't stop. Today you wear my marks. Today you're mine, Hallie. If they see, then they fucking *see*." He slapped me again, this time right on my pussy.

I screamed, arching back as his hand clamped around the stinging, swollen flesh. "Solace, please—"

"Is that what you want, Hallie, for me to give you relief?" Dark eyes glittered above me as his fingers sank deeper into my swollen, tingling flesh. "Beg for relief, Hallie. Beg for Solace."

My mind swirled as I parted my legs wider, words tumbling from my lips. "Please. Please, can I come, Solace. Please–" I gasped at another slap, this one softer, more playful.

"Rub against me," he ordered. "Show me how much you want it."

I whimpered, arching up to push myself against his fingers. *There.* That spot, right freaking *there.* "Oh, God," I cried, working my hips frantically. "Please, Solace," I gasped, tipping my head back, needing his mouth on mine.

His gaze bore into mine as his hand drifted away. "No."

I froze, mid-air hump. "What?"

"No." His smile was full of sin and an edge of cruelty I'd seen there before. "Fuck, girl. I might love you, but last night hurt. Today you ache for me, and tonight we fix this. Is that understood?"

I stared up at him, remembering his pledge that first night we walked to the bus together.

I'll teach you denial. How to cry for me.

As if called upon, a single tear dripped free from the corner of my eye. Satisfaction lit his face as he leaned down and licked it up.

"Fuck, you taste good," he murmured, finally caving and giving me the kiss I needed, holding my legs open but not touching me. "Tonight, beautiful. I promise. We will work this through together, okay?"

I nodded, sobbing out a gasp as he traced the marks he left on my inner thighs. "You won't let me change or wear tights, will you?" I asked, already knowing the answer and dreading it.

"No." That same smile played at the corners of his lips, possessive. Obsessive. "You are mine, beautiful. Now they'll know it." He straightened my seat, winding my seatbelt around me and tucked my hair tenderly behind my ears, all the while tracing the marks he left on me.

"So goddamn beautiful."

Somewhere in my heart, a warmth replaced the ache left there by fear so long ago. It was like if he kept saying it, I might actually start believing him.

CHAPTER SIX

SOLACE

The moment we parked out front of the Chimeras home building, I knew today was going to be all sorts of fucked up. Hux's head wave in my direction gave me advance warning, and I knew I screwed up by skipping practice. But when his gaze dropped to focus on Hallie, my happy moment dissipated.

"Wait here," I murmured, leaving her at my car, watching me with a frown as I jogged across the parking lot to meet Hux halfway. "Sorry I missed this morning Cap," I greeted him. "Had some shit to tidy up."

We didn't often get to call in a freebie, and it'd been years since I used one.

He rolled his shoulders. "Not about you."

I glanced over his shoulder at the door where Janelle had been loitering for the last week. "Where's your side piece?"

He shook his head. "Story for another time. Take her away for the day. Don't let her in." He glanced past me, his face tightening. "Fuck."

I looked over my shoulder at my car with no Hallie beside it. She must have headed around the back. I'd catch her in a second. "Damn. What's up?"

He passed over his phone. I scrolled through the photos, my gut tightening. There were snaps of Hallie and me in the sponsor's office earlier in the week, fighting. My hand was captured between her legs. Her head tipped back, bliss written across her face. Hell, the sight thickened my cock. Any other time I'd give into my own pleasure, but not like this. The next were at the gym, and I knew what they'd show.

"Who the fuck took these?"

Hux rolled his shoulders. "Dunno. We have a security issue, for sure. But man, her job's gone."

I stared at him, horror bringing my breakfast back up. Tossing his phone into his chest I turned on my heel, sprinting to the back of the building, but she was already inside.

"Hallie," I yelled. "Hallie!"

I headed for the kitchen, but changed my mind when I remembered I'd had her thermos refilled at a local cafe before she got up. She wouldn't need it. Pivoting on my heel I aimed for the office and knew what I'd find before I got there. Because I had a horrifying, sudden understanding of what happened, why she was so upset with me yesterday.

I gripped the office door and yanked it open to find the WAGS clustered around her, but the pictures weren't displayed on phones like I suspected. No, they'd taken it a step further.

They had projected the scenes I'd just viewed on Hux's phone onto the fucking wall.

Hallie, my private, introvert little Hallie, stared up at the pictures of the two of us together and they were beautiful. So goddam beautiful that she could be a model for any fucking company whether these women could see it or not. I sure as fuck knew the team saw it. A deep sound rose in my chest as I barreled my way into the office, pushing between ranks and slapping the back of more than one head who's owner had to adjust his pants when he couldn't take his eyes off the real thing.

"Let's get you out of here," I murmured in Hallie's ear, sliding my fingers around her arm.

She stood frozen, but when she turned to me, her face was devoid of emotion. "No."

"Huh?" I watched her carefully for signs of a breakdown, but the tears from when she talked about the asshole ex cheating on her weren't there. *Alright. Let's see how this plays out.* But the moment she hurt, I was taking her straight out of there. "What's on your mind, beautiful?"

"I'm not leaving," she said firmly, pressing her heels into the industrial grade carpet under her feet.

Hux burst through the front doors, the captain gone all gung-ho. His eyes trailed over the scene, over her, and the red marks I'd left visible on the inside of her thighs. He wasn't the only one to spot them, and the word *toy* made its rounds in the WAGS cluster in a not so subtle whisper, subtlety not really being their thing.

The Chimeras captain swallowed hard, raising his eyes to meet mine as he blew out a hard breath. *Get her out of here,* he mouthed.

I shook my head. *Her choice,* I replied, gripping her arm tight anyway. Despite my resolve and hers, if Hallie looked like she was going to crack, we were gone. If I had to pick her up to take her out, I'd do it and wear the consequences later. Anything for her. And I was an inch from calling it. Hell, the only reason I stayed was because she asked it of me.

"Whoever has the originals of these can hand them back, or delete them. Please," Hallie added in a clear, loud voice that stopped all conversation in the office.

"Damn, girl." I stared down at her, proud as motherfucking punch of the girl I loved who refused to be cowed by the pathetic attempt at bullying that had the opposite effect on every man in the room.

The corner of her mouth quirked. "I'm sure Solace would like them for personal use."

Hux laughed out loud, leaning back against the doors, barring exit in that direction. I nodded over my shoulder. Shannon took up position at the back of the room, trapping everyone inside.

"It doesn't matter." Janelle stepped out from behind her desk, her hair pulled into a demure ponytail, wearing the baggiest brown dress I'd ever seen on that woman. "She can't work here after that." She gestured to the mess on the wall where Hallie rode me in the gym.

Damn, I needed to remake that scene with her and have her clean the equipment with her tongue while I took her from behind.

I scoffed. "Are you fucking kidding me? You've

been screwing around with Hux for over a week, and before that every time you bent down, I got to say hello to your great-grandmother right along your gene line, *baby*," I tacked on with a sneer, belatedly noting her red-rimmed eyes and backed off the sarcasm an inch.

Hallie tilted her head to one side. "But she's not with Hux anymore, are you?"

Janelle stepped back, shook her head and retreated to her desk. "Do whatever you want, Hallie," she said in a small, tired voice, so unlike her usual outspoken personality that I stared.

But Hallie seemed to get it, still wrapped in her strange mood. "Did you meet Kylie Smart, Hux?"

The captain leaned away from the door, his show of bravado dropping. I squeezed her arm in warning.

"He came out to tell me," I murmured. "He's on your side."

"And I'm on his," she replied enigmatically, her voice lowered as she looked up at me, her eyes clear.

I studied her and nodded, ignoring the ongoing slideshow of us fucking overhead. Someone had the sense to stop the thing, and the room dimmed a little.

"Yes, actually, he did." The girl with the gold nails and the fake hair to match from the kitchen yesterday before Hallie went nuts on me sauntered across the room, sliding her arm through Hux's. She smiled brightly—too fucking brightly for the occasion—at everyone who gawked at the stranger in our midst. "I don't think he'll be playing with office girls anymore. You should probably reconsider, too," she said to me pointedly. "I've already removed her from one player before." She dismissed Hallie as though she was nothing, studying her gold, primped nails.

Hallie flinched.

All that show—the pictures of us fucking in full sight, the bullying, the words, the fat shaming in the lunchroom... everything, and *this woman* made her react?

The penny dropped for me in full. "You're the other woman." I stared at Kylie. "The puck bunny Hallie's ex cheated on her with."

Kylie didn't bother to look at me, intent on doing something with those damn talons attached to her fingers. Which meant she missed Hux's look of disgust aimed right at the top of her head.

Cap shook his arm free. "Get off me. And get the fuck out. I should have known better."

Kylie glanced up at him. "I'm sure you'll get over it. These things happen."

I straightened behind Hallie. "Cap said get out. You want me to ring security?"

Her eyes narrowed. "Want your photos back, big boy?"

"Fuck this." Hux dived into her bag, grabbed her phone, and tossed it to me. "That's yours now, man. Do what you need. I got this."

Kylie snarled at him as I texted security. It wouldn't hurt for a little back up. Hux didn't need a litigation case on his hands after everything. A wail went up from the side of the office. Hux sent an alarmed glance at Janelle who dissolved into tears at her desk as he escorted Kylie from the building under duress.

The door shut behind them. No one moved.

Well, no one, except for Hallie who took her coffee, the one I bought her before we got breakfast, and placed it in front of Janelle. "This one stays hot for hours. It's really good, too. I think Solace has good taste, but don't tell him. We should probably try to find that coffee shop later, okay? Go for a walk?"

Janelle lifted red rimmed eyes to meet Hallie's face and nodded with a trembling lip. "Okay," she whispered.

Hallie hugged her and I swore my heart exploded on the spot.

Somewhere in the back, one of the boys whistled. I promised myself I'd give him a reprieve of a day before I hunted him down.

Hux reentered the room, swept an inked hand through his hair, and offered me a tired nod. "She's banned from the grounds. Someone send a warning out to the other clubs about the show pony stalker before she infected them all, for God's sake."

"I'll do it." Hallie turned back to me and slid her arms around my neck. "Love you, too," she whispered in my ear softly, but somehow loud enough for the entire office to hear.

"Damn, I need to find a girl like that," Hux muttered soberly.

Not that I blamed him, but this one belonged to me, no matter how she called it. We could argue about semantics later. Hux nodded at Hallie. No one said anything as I picked her up and placed her ass on the chair that had been hers, though she was due a career shift in my opinion.

It looked like my girl kept her job *and* won some hearts at the same time.

Including mine.

EPILOGUE

HALLIE

I went home with Solace. Finally. He didn't beg after the catastrophe in the office. Actually, he didn't say much at all. Hux did, though, negotiate the pay rise and diagonal job shift I both appreciated and needed after the WAGS drama that got me right out of the main office and into the coaching department.

In my new role I'd report directly to Coach. Ward Bishop would be my direct boss from now on. The formidable Chimeras trainer glowered at Hux as the team captain laid out exactly why I now shared his space. I understood his mood shift—not that Ward Bishop had more than two, anyway.

No one else dared to invade his space either by choice or by design unless they were one of his team, and in shit at that. Yet here I stood between Solace and Huxley's combined bulk.

Ward observed me in utter silence for the better part of two minutes. I knew better than to fidget, having seen him discard wannabes from the team's reserve squad for less.

"She can stay if she can keep up with me."

Hux pressed his fingers gently between my shoulder blades in a show of support. "She'll keep up, sir," he murmured.

Ward's eyes narrowed. "And she needs to know the team's stats."

Solace's whole frame vibrated as he held in a laugh. "Better than any of us," he assured his coach.

My new boss's eyes fixed on me. Cold as the ice the boys skated on, silver hair dominated his temples in a sea of darkness. "I'm not some playboy like these kids, sweetheart. If you think you can waste my time, I assure you, we will be having a different sort of conversation you won't enjoy in short order."

I held his gaze. "I just told the WAG squad to take down the porn show they threw of me up on the office walls because I was sick of their bullshit. I couldn't get my work done with that crap going on. I'd appreciate someone who actually understands what work is, sir," I added, aiming for Hux's air of respect.

Ward's eyebrows rose. "Isn't that different?" he muttered.

Solace let out that laugh he'd repressed. The sound boomed around the rink. "Yes, sir. She is."

Which was how I ended up in the passenger seat of his car for the second time that day, headed for his place after we stopped in at mine so I could leave feed out for Mica. My hands tucked into my lap in a knot, I stared at the townhouses passing by in the shitty part of town I lived in near the commercial area where rent was cheap. Slowly the buildings moved into suburban homes, and then grew bigger. My heart stuttered as I took note of the luxury cars lining drives and the house frontages that took up more space than five of my townhouses.

"I think I'm in the wrong area," I choked, running my fingers along the door handle when Solace pulled up into a black bricked, electric gated drive.

An imposing, three story home set well back from the street with manicured gardens I knew Solace didn't look after himself surrounded me as he drove us deep into the property. The gates shut silently behind us, locking us in.

"You'll be fine." His hand closed around mine in a firm, warm grip.

"I can't afford to leave the car." *Or be in it.* I looked down at our tangled fingers. "Solace, I—"

He pulled his car up sharply on the dark gravel before the house and switched the engine off, turning to face me. "Come in so you can thank me for getting you a new job today. Then we can work on your punishment for fucking running from me when we arrived at the office and getting yourself into all sorts of trouble before I could be there to help you," he growled, wrapping his other hand around my wrist. He trapped both of my hands on either side of me against the base of the leather bucket seat.

I gasped out loud at both the indignity and the imprisonment. "I could have gotten myself that job with Ward. And Hux was there to help," I protested.

"But you got into trouble all by your fucking self, beautiful. I couldn't breathe. I worried about where you were, what they'd done to you. How much you'd hurt because of them." He rested his forehead against mine.

Coal dark eyes bore into mine as I stared back, struggling to breathe.

"I can look after myself," I whispered.

"But you don't have to. Not anymore, and not every time. I've got you. *We* have got you, beautiful," he murmured, and I knew he meant hum and Huxley. What they'd done this afternoon after I stood up for Hux with the not-WAG who shouldn't have been in the building in the first place.

I closed my eyes and breathed out. "Alright."

"Yeah?" He rubbed his nose against mine. "Gonna let me thank you and punish you tonight, welcome you to my place? Cause now you're here, you know I'm gonna want you to move you in."

I swallowed hard, keeping my eyes shut. He'd ask me to open them in a minute, and I would, but I wasn't ready just yet. "I know, Solace. Mica is a non-negotiable."

"Done." He kissed me swiftly, unbuckled my seatbelt and scooped his arms beneath me.

My eyes flung open as my massive hockey defender slithered out of the driver's seat and lifted me along with him.

"That should not have been possible. Or so easy."

"Leave the impossible things to me, beautiful. I've got plans for tonight that involve a pretty girl, whichever room in my house she chooses, and tearing those clothes off her." His fingers trailed along my body as he set me down. "The door's unlocked. Run, Hallie."

"The door's un– Who did that, and why?" I stared up at him, a frown twisting my lips as questions layered upon each other in my mind.

Solace stared down at me, not a smile in sight. "Run, beautiful. I'm faster than you think."

I stared for a second longer at his closed, formidable face. My heart rate picked up when he didn't move or say anything else. Just watched me like I was his next meal.

I knew this mood. This was the Solace who used to prowl across the parking lot when I left the Jericho Chimeras building each night when I started working with them.

From that first night when I wasn't sure if I'd end up in the back of the trunk just like the man who keyed Hux's car. But Solace kept his distance. Just watched, walked behind me, and then...he stopped. I got on my bus and I went home.

Every night after that, we repeated our same strange dance. Him watching me, me knowing he was there, until the night he approached me and our dance changed.

This was that mood only...tonight was nothing like that.

Run, beautiful.

I took one last look at those dark, hard eyes, already lost in shadow, and I ran.

Pivoted on my heel, dropped my bag and my files on the drive where they scattered like so much rubbish, and I sprinted.

He could have caught me at any time. I knew that. I didn't have a clue where the door to his house lay beyond the archway I spotted when we pulled up that disappeared into darkness. I headed toward that with a silent prayer. Behind me, gravel crunched as he walked—*walked*—after me. Long, slow steps that shot delicious, uncontrolled fear through me.

Come in so you can thank me for getting you a new job today. Then we can work on your punishment for fucking running from me.

Run.

That's what I did. Busted through the unlocked door he seemed to have planned, not caring if there was some employee in his house I might scare the living daylights out of as I found the foyer, the hallway, and the living area, then the kitchen in the world's fastest tour of Solace Hunter's home.

My legs shook as the front door shut. No, it slammed. I spun on the spot, found a new doorway and raced through it, only to find Solace hulking form on the other side, striding toward me.

I stared over my shoulder at where I swore the front door just shut. "But, the—"

"Run, Hallie." His teeth bared as he unbuttoned his shirt from the top down.

My feet didn't have the three second delay option my brain took, already moving up the curved stair-case I found through the next arched doorway. I took those two at a time, my thighs and lungs screaming in tandem. This office girl might work for the Chimeras, but she sure as hell wasn't one. Not in the fitness department.

Fingers caught at the hem of my skirt. I let out a yelp and powered through, really running now, in full flight mode. This might be Solace, but also—

This part of him scared me in all the best ways. He was huge and intimidating as shit.

I found a bedroom at a glance and a bathroom, bypassing both of those as options leading to instant doom. The next doorway looked like a hall. I turned it down and realised my mistake.

"My office. Interesting choice." Solace's hand closed around my waist. One hand, that's all it took. He squeezed my curves in an inescapable grip.

It took me less than a second to understand just

how sweetly Solace had been playing with me since he broke his vow of silence and approached me. His other hand slid up my front until his fingers caught my jaw and tipped my head back. Our eyes met, my panic and uncertainty meeting the raw, ravaging hunger in his.

"Solace—" I whimpered, my voice a bare thread, needy and pathetic.

"Fuck," he cursed, propeling us forward. My hips hit the edge of his desk. He bent me over the hardwood, pushing everything in front of me off the other side. Muted thuds announced heavy things meeting lux carpet. He didn't seem to care. "Christ, I can't think when you make sounds like that, Hallie. The things you do to my mind..." He hissed out a breath, releasing my jaw to rip my skirt up, grinding into me from behind. "At least here I don't have to worry about anyone else hearing you when you're in my home, or watching you. Though I do owe you a punishment."

"What for?" I clung to the desk's glossy, hardwood surface. My feet slid apart on the plush carpet beneath my feet when his boots tapped my legs open.

His hand slid between us, stroking my pussy through my panties still damp from our playtime early this morning. A moan left my lips as I leaned into his desk, tilting my hips up in a silent plea for more.

Solace froze. His touch disappeared. For an endless, impossible moment I thought I'd offended him.

"I'm sorry—" I started, with no real concept of what I was apologising for.

His palm came down on my panty-covered ass in a spank hard enough to bring tears to my eyes. "Fuck, there's those little moans that I love. Like I fucking love you." Another spank on the same side, then he switched.

I gasped between spanks, tried to breath but it took me a minute before he stopped, both of us panting as tears coated my face.

He leaned over my body, encompassing me with his bulk as he traced hair back from my face and kissed my cheeks. "I promised you a punishment. You did so well, beautiful. Fuck, today scared me. I didn't want to see you hurt."

"I was scared too," I admitted. "Terrified I'd have to walk out and never see you again. But you were there, and you stayed with me through it. After. That made it different to last time. I wasn't insignificant, and I wasn't forgotten. Passed over for someone... else," I finished.

His breath came hard as he worked at his pants. "Never gonna pass you over for anyone, beautiful. Never. Do you understand that?"

I didn't get a chance to say *yes* before he shoved my panties aside and thrust deep inside me. My scream bounced back at me from his study walls as he set a punishing pace. Solace's large, scarred hands gripped mine, stretching my body across his desk to the other side, and clamped my hands to the edge.

I struggled to breathe between the new position and his weight braced over me, how deep he drove inside me. His grip meant I couldn't let go, and I couldn't get away from him.

A second later, I was grateful for the support as he hammered into me, so brutal I thought I'd pass out. I couldn't keep up with his rhythm, barely breathing through each impossible thrust that bordered on painful.

Pleasure slammed me as I clung to the desk, glad he held me pinned to him for fear I'd be washed away beneath the onslaught of his desire.

My orgasm rolled through me with all the grace of an oncoming tsunami. It didn't stop there—or rather, it didn't stop at all. I screamed into the cold wood, my cheek turned to the side as my thighs trembled around his.

Solace's shout above me felt like that claiming I'd avoided for so long. But with him it was different. Maybe he had claimed me a whole lot longer ago, on that first night he watched me and walked behind me to the bus stop. My pussy clamped tight at the idea that I had been his for so much longer, milking his orgasm from him.

Bliss overwhelmed me as I trembled in his arms. Fluid gushed down my legs. My cheeks flushed at the added humiliation, but a large part of me didn't care. I was in his arms, his home with him. No matter how intense Solace Hunter could be, right now, with him wrapped around me, I was safe.

"I love you," I murmured against one massive, inked wrist, pressing my lips to his skin.

Solace's arms wrapped tight as he slumped over me, one fist braced on the desk beside my head.

"Fuck, I love you," he murmured, finding my mouth and kissing me deeply. "This is a forever thing, Hallie. The love, the overwhelm, playing, the punishments. I'm not ever gonna stop. Just...move the gray pussy in with me. And the white bedding. I still want pictures."

I giggled beneath him, trying to find enough space to fill my lungs. "I'd probably agree to anything right now," I admitted.

"I figured." He kissed me again. "We'll get to the punishment part later."

My breath hitched. "Wait, Solace—"

"We have got to talk about your avocado habit in the kitchens, beautiful."

READ THE BONUS SCENE

Thank you for reading Hallie and Solace's story.
I hope you loved this crazy couple as much as I do.
READ ON for a bonus epilogue
involving a little more denial on Solace's part.

MORE JERICHO CHIMERAS

Want more Jericho Chimeras?
Cap gets his girl (Hux!) in a second chance romance
in PUCK MY HEART
Read Shannon and Lori's can't-let-her-go story in
PUCK ME ALWAYS
on KINDLE UNLIMITED right now.

Sofia's Other Hockey Romances:
Crushing It
Glacial Force

ABOUT THE AUTHOR

USA Today Bestselling author Sofia Aves writes fast-paced police romances, sizzling military units, steamy cowboys with a Montana backdrop and the occasional cheeky god. Married to a veteran, she often tackles topics of PTSD and reintegration and has a soft spot for all who work in uniform. Sofia writes kidlit for charity and has over one hundred and fifty publications across four not-so-super-secret pen names.

Publishing is her life. As acquisitions editor for Evernight and Evernight Teen Sofia loves discovering new and established author voices in romance. She is a mum of three crazies in a returned veteran household and has a pair of overly large fur babies who think they're teacup puppies.

Sofia lives near Brisbane, Australia and has her own alpaca park, Lorendel.

www.sofiaaves.com

Sign up to Sofia's newsletter and get a free Blue Blooded Brothers book.

Haven't read the Z Boy's prequel? Get it for free here:

A TABLE FOR TEN

www.sofiaves.com

Follow Sofia on

Amazon

BookBub

Instagram

Goodreads

Tiktok

READ SOFIA'S SERIES

Blue Blooded Brothers
    Collision
    Politics & Paperwork
    Blindsided
    Sentinel
    Mugshots & Candy Canes
    Impact
    Reckoning

Red Hart Ranch
    Snow on the Range
    Siren on the Range
    Sundown on the Range
    Spirit on the Range
    Ash on the Range (2025)
    Mistletoe on the Range (2025)

Forgotten Mountain Man

Texan Devils

Ranger's Wish

Ranger Bedevilled

Ranger's Passion

Ranger's Fury

Ranger's Wrath

Ranger's Storm

Snapdragons & Seductions

Summer with a Ranger

Merry with a Ranger

Playing to Win

Off Boarding

Vicious Slash

Zero Pointer

Off Stage Fling

Rippton Allstars

Crushing It

Glacial Force

Rippton Creatives

Study Games

Make Me, Break Me

Twisted Obsession

Spring Break with a Mafia Prince

A Royally Fake French Menage

Jericho Chimeras

Puck Me Always

Puck My Heart

Puck me Sideways

Z Boys

King

Joker

Hearts

Ace

Mayhem & Mistletoe

Ruski

Fast Track to Love

Speed Trap

Klauss Brothers

Zander

Keegan

Gallo Empire *with Jade Marshall*

Splintered Vows

Fractured Vows

Fierce Vows

Savage Covenant

Rom Coms

She's A Hot Christmas Mess

Boats, Moats and Root Beer Floats

Writing Why Choose Dark Romance as

DOVE PRIEST

Recurve Ridge

Kidlit writing as

JO SEYSENER

The OCD Elf

writing YA as

JOSS PHOENIX

Alchem Academy (2025)

Writing spicy paranormal romance as

RAVEN HUSH

Club Fray

Darkest Desires

Purge

Kidnapped By Claws

Ruin

Shadow Lords

Sinner's End

Heaven's Gate (2026)

Monster Brides

Phoenix's Eternal Flame

Kraken's Vow

Krampus' Christmas Bride

Silent Sentinels Duet

Reflections of Silence

Echoes in the Void

Monsters In New York

Feral Moon Rising (2025)

Printed in Dunstable, United Kingdom